Land OF BROKEN PROMISES

Also by Jane Kuo
In the Beautiful Country

Land OF BROKEN PROMISES

JANE KUO

Quill Tree Books
An Imprint of HarperCollins Publishers

Quill Tree Books is an imprint of HarperCollins Publishers.

Land of Broken Promises
Copyright © 2023 by Jane Kuo
All rights reserved. Printed in the United States of America.
No part of this book may be used or reproduced in any manner
whatsoever without written permission except in the case of
brief quotations embodied in critical articles and reviews. For
information address HarperCollins Children's Books, a division of
HarperCollins Publishers, 195 Broadway, New York, NY 10007.
www.harpercollinschildrens.com

Library of Congress Control Number: 2023930321
ISBN 978-0-06-311904-8

Typography by Kathy H. Lam
23 24 25 26 27 LBC 5 4 3 2 1

First Edition

to Mom and Dad,

and to my children,
may you remember
where we have been

Land OF BROKEN PROMISES

March 29, 1982

Three minutes before the bell rings,
my books are neatly stacked.
Smear ChapStick, check.
Tuck hair behind ears, check.

Tiffany, my best friend, says
it's important to be just like everyone else,
with only one thing different.
She has red hair.
That's her one thing.

What's my one thing? I ask.
Oh, you're Asian, she says,
and leaves it at that.
As if being *Asian* is shorthand for so much.
But I know what she means.

My hair doesn't fluff and feather.
I don't have three-inch bangs
sitting on top of my forehead.

And the color, my hair's as black as squid ink.

I try extra hard to make sure
everything else about me is the same.
The same Pink Pearl eraser,
the same scratch-and-sniff stickers
on my Pee-Chee folders.

But there's always something just beyond my reach.
Now all the girls are wearing Jordache jeans,
while I'm still in hand-me-down Levi's.

Mark of Asia

Even at church there's this divide between the kids
who were born here,
called the American-born Chinese,
and the ones who were born somewhere else.
I'm the only one who was born in Taiwan.

Last year during Sunday school,
I wore a short-sleeved T-shirt
and dumb Kevin pointed to my arm, saying,
Someone has the mark of Asia.

I looked down to examine the two scars
left by the immunization shots
I had as a baby.

What does that mean? I asked.

Kevin said that Americans
don't have scars on their arms
and it's a telltale sign that *you weren't born here.*

I couldn't think of a swift reply
before Miss Chen started the Sunday school lesson.
I was distracted and sad the rest of class
because the *mark of Asia*
meant I could never be an American spy,
since anyone could tell
just by looking at my arm
that I wasn't born here.

It was another sign
that I'll never be a real American.

Uncomfortable Laugh

Tiffany's a real American.
An entire wall of her house
is filled with family portraits.
There's Great-Grandma Speer,
and Great-Grandpa Bailey.
Mrs. Nagel says one side of her family
fought in the Civil War.
I don't ask her which side they were on.

She points.
*Here's a photo of my great-great-grandfather
in his woodworking studio.*

Then she asks about my family.
What did your ancestors do?

They were farmers, I say,
and there's this awkward pause
as she waits for me to say more.
Except there's nothing else to say.

5

They were farmers all the way down to my grandfather
on Ma's side, my *a gong*.
He was a farmer and a barber.

She asks if I have any photos
of my great-grandparents.

No, no, I don't, I reply.
Mrs. Nagel looks sad,
so I say, *That's okay.*
If there ever was a photograph
of my great-grandfather at work
it would be of him standing in a rice paddy,
knee deep in muddy water.

Mrs. Nagel laughs.
But it's an uncomfortable *ha ha*.
I can tell, she doesn't think it's funny at all.

I guess I do feel kind of bad
that I don't have any pictures of my great-grandparents.
But mostly, I'm sad it's just the three of us here
and that all our relatives are either in China or Taiwan.

We're the only ones in America
and we're not even American.

Black

In Mr. Hollander's art class,
there's a poster of *Werner's Nomenclature*,
colors and the names of colors.
Pyrite, saffron, honey, primrose, and *sulfur*
are just some of the names for yellow.

There are four different places associated with blue,
and I don't know what makes a particular shade
Prussian, Berlin, Scotch, or *China.*

Mostly, though, I want to know,
who is Werner and why does he get to name colors?

Because some of his names suck.
All the blacks are just variations of the same *ish*:
greyish, greenish, brownish black.

Mr. Hollander tells us,
There are even some people who say
black is not a color.

7

It's the absence of color.
Black absorbs all color
and reflects none of it back.

But black is a color!
I spend the rest of the period
thinking of names:
charcoal
obsidian
ebony
ash
raven
burnt
midnight.

Two Classrooms

Most sixth graders just have one teacher
that they stay with all day.
And from that one person they learn:
English
history,
math,
and
science.
Then twice a week,
we all go to Mr. Hollander for art
and Mrs. Bauer for PE.

I'm lucky I have two teachers:
Mrs. Matthews for English and history
and Mr. San Filippo for math and science.

Mrs. Matthews says she traded all the math and science
she's responsible for to Mr. San Filippo.
She says, *This way, I get to teach what I love.*

So my day is split in half
between two classrooms
and I like both:
math and science,
English and history.

I'm glad I don't have to choose.

Before

It's not just the outside,
the way I look,
the particular shade of my obsidian hair.
It's everything about me,
where I'm from,
my family,
the fact that Ma and Ba own a store
and I work there after school.

I wasn't always so different.
I used to be just like all the other girls
in a sea of blue-and-white uniforms.
We even wore the same brand of white ankle socks.
That was before, in Taiwan.

The truth is, even then we were different.
Ma and Ba dreamed of *the beautiful country*.
It wasn't unusual to dream,
but Ma and Ba made that dream a reality.
We left Taiwan a year and a half ago

and settled in Duarte.

Ba came over first
and bought Dino's, our store.
Then Ma and I came over, a hundred days later.
We brought along six suitcases
and left everything else behind.

Work

Almost always, the first thing I do
when I get to the store is make myself a drink.
The options are:
Coke
Diet Coke
7UP
Dr Pepper
Orange Fanta
Mountain Dew

It's not just those six choices
because with a soda dispenser,
I can mix and match.
Coke and 7UP in equal parts,
7UP with just a splash of orange Fanta,
or is it a just plain old Mountain Dew kind of day?

There are so many possible combinations.
Ma showed me how to do the math.
It's six factorial,

which is six with an exclamation point.
To get the answer,
you multiply 6 x 5 x 4 x 3 x 2 x 1.
That's 720 different drink combinations!

I think today I'll go for Coke and Dr Pepper.
The science is getting the mixture just right,
not too much or that licorice taste
from Dr Pepper overwhelms the Coke.
Also, it's important to measure the ice-to-soda ratio.
Too much and I risk an ice cream headache,
too little and the drink won't be cold enough.

I'm just about to sit down with my soda,
when Ma asks,
When are you going to start working?

I'm here.
I'm at work, I reply.

I take my first sip of soda.
Perfect!
If only Ma wasn't standing here, hovering.

Ma says,
Ai Shi, being at work is not the same as working.

When you're done with your drink,
go prepare the lettuce.

Okay, okay. I tell her.

What I really want to say is this:
I don't work hard because you don't pay me to work.

But that's a fight for another day.
I take two more sips
and then carry my drink to the back.
Time to prep the lettuce.

Hired Hand

It's been a point of tension
between the three of us this whole year,
whether or not I get paid
for working at the store.

Whenever I'd hint that they should give me extra money
beyond my piddly allowance of two dollars a week,
Ba would say,
You are a contributing member of the family.
We don't want you to feel like a hired hand.
You're our daughter,
and we'd never insult you
by paying you to work.

I'd smile and nod
but inside, my head was doing somersaults
as I silently screamed,
Insult me, please!

Ba wasn't trying to get out of giving me money.
This is just how he thinks.

Then Ma would say,
I want to pay you.
After all, a good worker deserves her wages.
The question is, Ai Shi,
are you a good worker?

She'd glance toward the restroom,
the place where I'd go hide whenever
there were onions that needed to be cut,
or when the floor needed mopping,
or when it was time to take trash out
to the smelly dumpster.

And I'd reply, my cheeks hot with shame,
No, no, you don't need to pay me.
I'm not some hired hand.

Baby

The store isn't really a store,
it's a fast-food place
that used to just serve American food:
burgers, fried chicken, and BBQ ribs.
Then Ma and Ba added Taiwanese food to the menu:
five-spice ribs, fried rice, and egg rolls.

The store is the most precious thing we own.
The front half is covered almost entirely in glass:
shiny, fragile, and breakable,
like a jewelry box.

Ma says the store is her work
and Ba's work,
their hobby,
life savings,
retirement fund,
investment property,
and college savings
all rolled into one.

I add one more thing onto the list.
The store is also a baby,
Ma and Ba talk about the store as if she's a person
that needs to be taken care of,
the baby of the family.

Because the one thing we cannot do is close the store.
Not even when I'm singing in the choir concert at school,
or it's science night,
and I've been awarded first prize for my project,
Do the chemicals in a perm change the color of your hair?

Someone always has to stay with the baby.

Sit or Stand

Whenever we talk about the future,
Ma and Ba say,
You can be anything you want.
Just work in an office,
at a big desk,
where you sit all day.

Don't be like us,
we have to stand.

So, *either doctor or lawyer.*
You get to choose.

Sea Captain

You can be anything you want, he says.

But in the beautiful country,
Ba no longer does what he wants.

I look at photos of him from before.
He's standing on the deck of a ship
in a crisp white uniform.
He's not standing at attention,
because he's the one everyone else is saluting.
Ba is the captain.

Just last week, we added fish and chips
to the menu at Dino's.

I asked him,
When you were a sea captain,
did you fish much?

Ba huffed,
My job was to transport cargo, not catch fish.
Then he walked away,
not wanting to talk anymore.

It was Ma who asked me later,
Did you picture your father
sitting at the bow of a boat holding a fishing rod,
with all the time in the world?

I nodded.

Ma said,
Your father was the captain of a ship
that carried millions of dollars' worth of cargo
all over the world.
It was only after you were born that he stopped sailing,
because he didn't want to be away from you.

I asked her,
What else do I not know about him?

Ma turned away as if lost in
a long-forgotten memory.
She said, *Your father can navigate the world*
by the light of the stars.

Latchkey Kid

Ever since that conversation with Ma
about Ba on a cargo ship,
I've been pretending that I'm Pippi Longstocking.
She's a girl on TV
who lives alone for months at a time
while her sea captain father is away.
It's just her and a horse and a pet monkey.
Her world is free from the glare of adults.

I only pretend I'm Pippi Longstocking
when Ma and Ba let me stay home alone on Tuesdays,
when the store isn't so busy
and they don't need me to work.
That's when I become what Hal Fishman
of KTLA's nightly news calls a *problem*,
because I'm a kid at home
without any adult supervision.
And it's happening to so many of us
there's even a name for it.
We're called *latchkey kids*.

I wonder what Hal Fishman would say if he knew
that Tuesdays when I'm a latchkey kid
is when I most feel like a regular kid.

Fun

Today, instead of going home,
I go over to Tiffany's house.

Ba doesn't like that I go over there so much.
He believes in something called reciprocity.
He says that since an adult is almost never at our place,
and I can't invite Tiffany over,
I shouldn't go over to her house so much.

But Ma likes it when I go over to the Nagels'.
She says, *It's nice for you to have fun
every once in a while.*

When she says that
I'm both happy and sad,
because she really does want me to be like other kids,
without a care in the world,
and yet she knows that most of the time,
I'm not a regular kid at all.

Cheese Sprinkles

Tiffany's house is the second American home
I've been in.
The first house belonged to Terry and Don
and their girls.
They were our only friends for the longest time,
and then in January, the Eatons moved away,
back to Ohio.

And I know it's kind of silly
but I can't figure out if the Nagels are rich or not.
I mean, just like the Eatons,
they have a lot of stuff,
heavy wood furniture, a humongous TV,
and Tiffany even has a waterbed,
which means she sleeps on a plastic mattress
filled with water.
It sounds fun, but just sitting on that thing
for two minutes makes me seasick.

Whenever I go to Tiffany's house after school

I can almost always expect an invitation
to stay for dinner.
Sure enough, while we're trying to solve
the Rubik's Cube,
Mrs. Nagel asks,
Would you like to stay for dinner, Anna?
We're having spaghetti.

Yes, thank you, I reply.

Tiffany and I set the table.
Tall glasses of milk
for the two of us and her brother, Trevor.
Napkins, matching plates,
the sense of order and symmetry,
each item paired with its twin,
salt and pepper, spoon and fork.

The best part of Mrs. Nagel's spaghetti
is the green canister of cheese sprinkles
that gets passed around.
Trevor shakes so much onto his plate
the red sauce barely peeks through.
I do the same.

Dinner becomes this little performance
where I pretend I'm an American.
No elbows on the table,
and absolutely no slurping,
even though in Taiwan
slurping noodles is considered a compliment.
I twirl a forkful of spaghetti against a spoon
and then stuff the whole thing in my mouth.

How was school today, girls?
Mr. Nagel asks.

Fine, we answer in unison, and giggle.

What are your summer plans, Anna?
Mr. Nagel asks.
I glance up to see if Mr. Nagel really wants to know.
His bushy eyebrows are raised up
and there's the slight curl of a smile.
He's waiting for an answer.

I dab the corners of my mouth
with a napkin to buy time.

I'll probably do the same thing I did last year, I say.
Then, to change the subject,

I ask for the cheese sprinkles
and give another three shakes onto my plate.

For the rest of dinner,
I'm here but I'm not really here.
I'm thinking about summer
and how I don't have any plans at all.

Rank Order

I'll probably just work.

Ma and Ba don't know about summer camps
or classes at the YMCA,
or maybe they do know but don't bring it up
because those things cost money.
Also, they like having an extra set of hands at the store.

Ugh.
What I really want to do is go back to Taiwan.
It'll be almost two years since we left
and I'd love to see my relatives,
especially my grandparents and my cousin, Mei.
And I wouldn't mind pigging out
on yummy Taiwanese food.

Even though Ma and Ba
have never said,
You can't go back,
I can piece it together:

they would never send me on plane by myself
and besides, plane tickets are expensive.
I know better than to ask.

My second choice would be summer camp.
Tiffany's going to Big Bear Lake.
That sounds expensive too.

My third choice is the Chinese Camp
that a bunch of kids from church go to.
During the school year,
those same kids also go to Chinese Saturday school.
They complain about it all the time
and tell me I'm so lucky I don't have to go,
but secretly I wish I could go because
at least Chinese Saturday school would break up
the monotony
of being at the store all the time.

My fourth choice would be to stay home,
pretend I'm Pippi Longstocking and watch a lot of TV.
Adrian Van Roaltan, my science lab partner,
says that in the summer,
Channel 5 airs *Star Trek* and *Twilight Zone* marathons
for eight hours straight.

Finally, my last choice,
which isn't really a choice at all,
is to work at the store
the whole summer,
for no pay.

Beach

There's one more thing on my list for the summer,
and that's the beach.

My classmates go all year round.
Even though it's March and technically still winter,
Dorene and Agnes are talking about their
weekend plans,
visiting beaches with names like
Redondo, Malibu,
Santa Monica,
Huntington, Manhattan,
and Venice.

I was born in Hualien, a beach town.
I used to swim in the ocean almost every weekend.

If I had stayed,
I would have learned how to surf by now,
but here in sunny Southern California,
I have not seen the ocean this whole time.

When I look at all the blues
in *Werner's Nomenclature of Colours,*
I can't find the blue ocean of my memory.

Already and Not Yet

Mr. San Filippo, my science teacher,
is off on one of his tangents.
He's been going strong for fifteen minutes.

He says,
Did you know the Inuit people
have over fifty different words for snow?
You can tell what's important to a people
by the sheer number of names they have for things.

I believe it.
Like in Southern California,
we even have a name for the wind
that blows in from the desert, the Santa Anas.

And Ba has so many different names for America.
For the longest time,
we called America by its Mandarin name,
Mei Guo, which means *beautiful country*.
Then towards the end of last year,

Ba started calling this place *the promised land*.

I think he heard that phrase
from one of Pastor Chiang's sermons.
I remember the pastor saying,
The Israelites have left slavery in Egypt
but have not yet entered the promised land.
They are living in the already and the not yet.

That was when Ba began to call America
the land of milk and honey,
the place that God has given us to make a home,
the promised land.

But even Ba will be the first to admit,
this place hasn't always lived up to its name.

Sometimes,
when I feel the Santa Anas,
and see the thin layer of silt
brought in by the desert wind,
I think, maybe we're not in *the promised land* at all.
Because before the people of God
entered the land of milk and honey,
they had to wander the desert for forty years.

I wonder if we're actually in the desert,
wandering, waiting,
in the land between already and not yet.

Light

We stand to sing, we sit.
My skirt swishes the back of my knees.

Today we're in *big church*
for the first Sunday of the month.
That's when all of us are together,
kids and adults.
And while all the other kids squirm
and roll their eyes and complain,
the secret is, I kind of like *big church*.

Us kids, we can't just sit anywhere.
We have to sit with our parents,
because last summer Kevin got caught
passing notes during the sermon
and then Adam was in trouble for sneaking in
a wad of Big League Chew.
I swear the choir director's neck vein popped out an inch
when he saw us with our chipmunk cheeks
full of bubble gum in the back pew.

But even without the note-passing
and the bubble-gum chewing,
I like *big church*.

I sit in the quiet,
watching the sun filter in
through the church's cloudy glass windows.
It's the same light peeking
through the mountains above Duarte.
I feel the same sense of awe,
the same smallness,
and for a moment,
I allow myself to be seen.

American Car

Ever since Mr. San Filippo told us
about all the different words for snow,
I've been thinking about cars,
all the names Americans have for cars:
sedan, pickup, hatchback,
four-door, Chevy, Pinto,
Cadillac, Beemer, Benz,
Honda, Impala, and so on.

Today, we don't head over
to the Chinese grocery store
in Monterey Park after church.
Instead, we ride the bus to the Buick dealership.

We buy a car!

It was important to Ba that we buy American.
Even though a Japanese car would have been cheaper,
he wanted something *Made in the USA,*
because he loves this country.

Ba is the one who convinced Ma.
He said, *We live in America now,*
and I want to show our love
and loyalty by buying American.

Ma said okay because it was rare for Ba
to want to spend more money.
That's how she knew it was important to him.

It's important to me too.
We're in the Buick driving home
at thirty-five miles per hour along Route 66.

I'm in the car
but I'm also outside the car, looking in.
I see a girl sitting in the back seat,
window rolled down,
wind in her hair.
She's thinking,
Today is the closest I've come
to be becoming a real American.

Words

Mrs. Matthews, my English teacher, has a rule.
Anyone, at any time, can go look up a word
in the dictionary
even if she in the middle of a lesson,
even if her mouth is open mid-sentence.
That's how much Mrs. Matthews wants us
to use the dictionary,
because words are power.

I walk to the back of the room,
where the *Oxford English Dictionary* is on a stand
that looks very much like the pulpit
Pastor Chiang preaches from on Sundays.

And because there are so many words
in the English language
and the print is tiny,
the dictionary comes with its own magnifying glass.

I pick up the glass
and lean into the word
zephyr,
asking the OED,
What do you have to tell me?
as if she was a friend,
spilling a secret.

Destiny

If Ba had his way,
he'd be flipping burgers with a spatula in one hand
and holding a book of poetry in the other.
His favorite poems are the ones
written a thousand years ago,
during the Tang dynasty.

If I had my way,
my nose would be stuck in a book too.
Ba and I have this in common.
But it wouldn't be a book
of thousand-year-old Chinese poems.

My Chinese is fading.
The words I use,
the words I love,
are in English,
and they are my own,
separate from Ma and Ba.

It shouldn't be a surprise to Ma and Ba
that I'm this way,
because they're the ones who named me *Ai Shi*.

Ai means love,
Shi is poetry.

Ma and Ba didn't consult a baby name book.
They considered the entire language
and chose two words to be my name.

Telling someone your Chinese name
is giving them a glimpse into the hopes and dreams
your parents had when they named you.
Because names are destiny.

Cuts Both Ways

But a part of me doesn't want
to love a language that is so slippery,
a language that separates me from my parents.

English is a very strict gatekeeper.
As much as I have been welcomed in,
the gates slam shut when Ma and Ba try to enter.
The door is locked,
and it's not just one lock but many.

There's grammar,
with its rules,
and then the exceptions to those rules.
There's vocabulary,
when the sheer number of words overwhelms,
and there's the most difficult lock of all, pronunciation.

My parents even mispronounce the word *pronunciation*.

Doctor or Lawyer, Part One

They say,
You can be anything you want,
but they have preferences.

Ba wants me to be a lawyer.
And even though Ma named me Ai Shi,
she hates it when I read at the store.
When Ma catches me reading
when I'm supposed to be working,
she says, *Pretty stories can't fill an empty stomach.*

She wants me to be a doctor
because she likes math and science.

Mostly, I can't imagine a job is something you like doing.
I think lots of adults secretly think *work sucks.*

I mean, look at Ma and Ba.
They don't seem to enjoy owning a fast-food restaurant.
And I see it in the faces of our customers too,

the ones who sigh every Friday, *TGIF*.

But if I had to choose,
I think I want to be a lawyer when I grow up,
because I love words,
even though I've never even met a lawyer.

Statue of Liberty

Most teachers just stick to the curriculum,
like marking off the checkboxes on a to-do list.
Not Mrs. Matthews.
She has us study stuff that's not on the list.
There's this whole section on the hidden parts
of California history.
She talks about the vaqueros of the American West,
the Chinese who built the railroads,
and the people detained on Angel Island.

Mrs. Matthews teaches both English and history,
which means sometimes
she combines the classes
and uses literature for a history lesson or vice versa.

Today we're reading the poem
that's at the foot of the Statue of Liberty,
written by Emma Lazarus.

"Give me your tired, your poor,
Your huddled masses yearning to breathe free,
The wretched refuse of your teeming shore.
Send these, the homeless, tempest-tost to me,
I lift my lamp beside the golden door!"

Here's our assignment:
write a poem addressed to Ms. Lazarus
as if you were having a conversation with her.
So I write:

Ms. Emma Lazarus,
what would you say now,
if you saw me today,
standing on the teeming shores
of New York City,
yearning to breathe free?

Would you tell me I smell like fish?

What would you say
to my parents after taking one good look at their faces
and hearing their broken English?

What would you say to my parents,
who have had to work so hard?

Ms. Lazarus, you wrote your poem in 1883.
Did you know that the year before,
Congress passed the Chinese Exclusion Act of 1882?

Do you want to add a parenthesis to your poem?
Go ahead, I'll wait.

The bell rings.
I tear the sheet of paper
out of my notebook,
deposit my poem
into the wooden tray on my way out the door.

I never knew writing poetry could be so much fun.

Funny Ha-Ha

The next day,
Mrs. Matthews is wearing a Mona Lisa smile,
arms crossed, her eyes trailing me
as I walk into class.

Oops, maybe I made a mistake.

I slouch the entire time,
low into my seat.
When class is over,
I sprint to the door,
and just when I think I'm free, I hear,
Oh Anna, Anna Zhang,
can I talk to you?

Darn!
It's lunchtime, so I can't even pretend
I'll be late for my next class.

Yes, Mrs. Matthews?

I'm standing next to her desk.
A layer of papers on it, one inch thick.

You're funny, she says.

I'm quiet even as I'm wondering,
funny ha-ha or funny strange?

She keeps talking.
You have a way with words.

Her Mona Lisa smile broadens.

Oh, thank you?
Is this about my poem, Mrs. Matthews?
I was just having fun, I reply.

Yes, I know you were having fun,
and I had fun reading it.
When you go to junior high next year,
I want you to check out the Speech Club.
I think you'd really like it.
Mr. Hernandez is a good friend of mine,
and I bet he'd love to have you join.

Okay, thank you, Mrs. Matthews, I reply.

Think about it, and if you're interested,
you can even work on the speech over the summer.
The prompt is "What America Means to Me."
Here's the sheet with all the information.

Thank you.
I take the sheet of paper
and walk out of class, wondering,
What does America mean to me?

Contract

He comes by on a Saturday morning
because Ba told him we have to be at work by ten.

He comes by with his son.
They don't take off their shoes,
even though our shoes are neatly lined up
against the front door,
and our thin-socked feet look so small
next to their leather-clad feet.

We own the land that the store sits on.
It's ours, but we rent the apartment.
Litchfield is here with his son
to negotiate the terms of the new lease.

Both of them are wearing button-up shirts
and striped ties.
They have leather briefcases to match
their leather shoes.

Litchfield begins with small talk.
How do you like living here?

Ba answers his question with one sentence replies.
We like living here very much.

How's work? Litchfield asks.

Work is going well.

Then Litchfield points to his son.
This is my son, a lawyer.
He went to Harvard Law.
He's working with me in the family business.

Before I can shake my head,
before I can give Ba's arm a quick squeeze as if to say,
Please don't, it's too late.
Ba says, *Oh, my daughter wants to be a lawyer.*

The landlord's eyes twinkle.
Harvard Law smiles.
I keep my head very still
while my eyes dart around looking
for a big rock to hide under.

Harvard Law takes out a thick packet
from his briefcase and places it on the table.
The landlord says, *This is the contract.*

It's bigger than a week's packet of math homework,
and the type is only slightly larger than
words in the *Oxford English Dictionary*.

Ba doesn't have his glasses for reading fine print,
so Ma has to go get them.
Harvard Law and his father just sit there
staring at Ba as he reads the lease.

I just sit there too.
My eyes settle on Harvard Law's briefcase.
It's black and heavy
and the leather is so shiny,
it looks like a shield.

Dumb-Dumbs

Ba finishes reading the contract.
I can tell he still doesn't fully understand.
When he reads English, he almost always needs
to have a dictionary nearby.

He signs it anyways.
What choice does he have?

Later, he asks me,
What does this mean?
pointing to a paragraph in the contract.
I explain as best as I can.

Then, a few minutes after that, he asks,
What about this?

I do my best to explain
the diligent performance of tenant's obligations.

We read through all the extra attachments

called *addendums*.
We begin by learning how to pronounce the word,
uh den dm.

There's the waterbed addendum,
the pet addendum,
and the termination on sale of premises addendum.

Ma, eavesdropping on our attempt at
deciphering the terms of the lease, exclaims,
Wah, so many a-dumb-dumbs!

Doctor or Lawyer, Part Two

Ba's never been very good at filing paperwork.
The lease sits on the kitchen table for days.
I stare at the contract,
amazed that words on a page
can have so much power.

Well, it doesn't matter.
We have the store, and if anything ever happens
with Litchfield and Harvard Law,
we can rent another apartment, anywhere, anytime.

But the apartment is our home,
and now there's this unsettling feeling,
knowing that something called *the law*
can force us to move.

Now I see how lawyers can be like bullies.
Only they push people around with words,
instead of muscles.
And there's a part of me that wants to be a bully,

especially a bully who wears a suit
and sits at a big desk
and gets paid lots of money.

But doctors get paid a lot too,
and they get paid per patient.
The faster they can see a patient,
the more money.

The only thing is,
I haven't been to a doctor in a while,
and it seems kind of hypocritical
to want to be a doctor
when I don't even go to the doctor's anymore.

Unless you count the guy at church
who drives a Mercedes the color of margarine.
That's the only time we ever see a doctor,
even when we need to see one.

Dr Pepper

We have a shoebox to hold medicine
from the Chinese pharmacy.
Little brown pills for upset stomach.
Gou Pi Yao Gao, a stinky salve
that Ma softens over a flame
and applies to strained muscles.
There's also *Yunnan Bai Yao*,
which literally means *white powder from Yunnan*.
Ba sprinkles that over cuts and scrapes.
And for the last year and a half,
there was no health problem
that little shoebox couldn't solve.

Until last month,
when Ma had a fish bone stuck in her throat.
She kept coughing and coughing,
to clear her throat.

keh keh keh

When I heard her cough,
I'd swallow,
grateful that I didn't have a fish bone
stuck in my throat.

Then I felt guilty for being grateful.

For two days,
Ma walked around with her forehead knotted in worry.
Ba told her, *We have money.*
Let's take you to see a doctor.

Ma said, *Just one more day.*
Because she knew we didn't have that much money
and she didn't want to close the store.

Then, on the third day,
her forehead was no longer knotted,
she no longer coughed every few minutes.

It's gone, she said.

That's when Ba began to say,
Doctors are a luxury.
He would take a swig of soda,
point to the Dr Pepper in his cup,

and say, *That's the only doctor I need.*

When I asked him,
What about lawyers?

Ba said, *Oh, a good lawyer*
can mean the difference between life and death.
Then he laughed.
It was a strange laugh,
a little too loud,
for a little too long.

Too Much

After church, we take the car
to Monterey Park's Diho Market.

Ma grabs a bag of dried shiitake mushrooms
the size of a large pillow.
She grabs half a dozen cans of bamboo shoots,
jars of pickled cucumbers and radishes,
fresh bitter melon, eggplant, bok choy, and watercress.
There's a watermelon as big as a pregnant lady's belly,
papaya, and a five-pound sack of oranges.

Ba pulls two earthenware jars of stinky tofu
off the shelf,
and there are special treats just for me:
candied winter melon, haw flakes, White Rabbit candy.

We're greedy because now we have a car
and we don't have to lug everything onto the bus.
We buy so much food, too much.

We get home,

empty the bags of groceries onto the kitchen table.

Not everything can fit into the refrigerator and cabinets.

Ma turns around and around.

She sees a cabinet

right above the refrigerator,

a spot she's never noticed before.

There, that's the perfect place for the shiitakes, she says.

Ma stands on a chair and opens the cabinet.

It's not empty at all.

It's full of papers.

Piles

There are weekly mailers from the grocery store,
letters from credit card companies,
flyers from the elementary school.

Ma doesn't finish putting the groceries away.
She stops and sorts through the mail,
while the bok choy wilts
and the bitter melon
sits on the kitchen table, hardening.

It's all the mail from our first year here,
she says, flipping through the mass of paper.

Ma and Ba had a deal.
He was the one in charge of the mail and paperwork,
anything that involved reading English.
She was the one in charge of the kitchen,
both at home and at the store.

Now I remember how, for the longest time,
the mail was piled up in the corner,
next to the window,
where the Christmas tree used to sit.

Riddles in Small Type

This is what I think happened.

He must have thought, *Why bother?*
Most of it was junk anyways, which was true.
Supermarket flyers, advertisements,
Pennysaver mailers, coupons, and letters.

Maybe the idea of having to sit there
and read all that mail
with only a Chinese/English dictionary
to keep him company was just too much.
English is such a slippery language,
and even with a dictionary,
English words are like riddles in small type.

That first year,
after the break-ins started,
he was so tired,
and he couldn't stand the thought
of sorting through paper.

So, he tried to keep the pile neat.
The swirl of mail,
one pile becomes two piles,
and if two,
then why not three?
The piles collapse, mix
and mingle back into one big pile
until one day he's sick of looking at it.

He decides to *do something*.
He stuffs the mail into the cabinet
above the fridge, where it sits waiting,
until now.

Arrivals and Departures

Ma sifts through all the paper.

Hidden in all that junk is a sheet of paper
from the Immigration and Naturalization Service.

Ma holds the document up to his face.
What's this?

I watch as Ba's eyes travel down
the length of the paper.
He reads every word.
He doesn't need a dictionary at all.

He says,
It's about our immigration visa,
specifically the I-94 document,
which tracks our arrival and departure.
The document states that unless we apply for a new I-94,
we have to exit the country by January 14, 1981.

Today is May 2, 1982.

Status

Now I hear the words
yi min shen fen all the time.

I know *yi min* means immigration.
They had to tell me
shen fen means status.

Now that our I-94s have expired,
Ba and Ma worry about our *immigration status*.

Grief

The school counselor is giving a presentation
on how to handle life's disappointments.

She says, *Dr. Elisabeth Kübler-Ross developed*
a framework to help us understand
all the stages of grief we go through:
denial,
anger,
bargaining,
depression,
acceptance.

I read through the different stages
and I see *Werner's Nomenclature of Colours.*
Denial is *sienna yellow*
from the stamens of a honeysuckle.
Anger is the red heat of *arterial blood.*
Bargaining is the color of Ma's shirt,
a dark, purple-tinged green,

from *the leaves of woody nightshade*.
Depression is hard and gray, *flint*.

And the color of acceptance is blue,
the blue of the ocean,
the color I long for.

Third Day

After Ma found the letters,
she spent two days yelling,
while Ba was the quiet one, the calm one,
the one who didn't have to say anything,
because how can one reason with an angry person?

It was like a dance,
even though neither of them knew how to dance.
Ma would yell, demand answers.
Ba would retreat behind a stony wall of silence.
Until she went too far
and said or did something
she regretted.

And because Ma was ashamed
of what she said or did,
a word that cut like a knife,
a broken plate that flew out of her hand,
she was the bad one.

Ba could just stand back
and watch that part of her solo performance,
and he never had to answer the question,
How could you let this happen?

She screamed for two days
and then she stopped screaming
because she didn't want to drown in her own sorrow
or because she had nothing left.
I'm not sure which.

On the third day, she said to Ba,
I forgive you.
We can't undo the past.
We have to move forward.

From then on,
she set her mind on figuring out
how to get the paperwork in order.
She said with a lilt in her voice,
It's not that bad.
We can fix this.

I really wanted to believe her.

Library Books

I'm in the school library, thinking
about overdue books.

Maybe the Immigration and Naturalization Service
treats due dates like a suggestion,
the same way Mrs. Thompson, our librarian,
treats overdue books.

Maybe the INS is kind and flexible
like Mrs. Thompson.
Last year, when I really wanted to keep
my *Ramona the Pest* book for one more week
because I was a slow reader and just learning English,
Mrs. Thompson let me hold on to it.

There are no fines at the school library
for turning in a book late.
The regular public library has fines,
but it's only a nickel for kids' books
and even then, the maximum fine is a dollar.

Maybe the government will only fine us
a dollar for the expired paperwork.

Thirty-One Flavors

Ma found a lawyer
who might be able to help us.

She's on the phone with her now,
while Ba and I stand by, waiting.

I ask Ba,
Is this lawyer like that other lawyer we met,
the landlord's son?

No, this one specializes in immigration law.

Oh, I didn't know there are lawyers just for immigration.

Ba replies,
There's a different lawyer for every problem you have.
It's like that ice cream place, thirty-one flavors.

Ma gets off the phone and tells us,
She's willing to meet with us.

Only problem is the earliest available appointment
is at the end of August, three months from now.

So what now? I ask.

We wait.
This gives us time to get
the money together to pay her,
if she takes our case.

How much? Ba asks.

Three thousand dollars.

I'm silent,
letting that number sink in.
We don't have that kind of money,
especially not after buying the Buick.
The store only makes $150 to $200 a day,
and that's before paying for utilities and supplies.

Undone

There's a well of sadness about
what Ba left undone.

I walk to the back of Mrs. Matthews' class
and flip open to the *R*'s.

Rupture, noun
an instance of breaking or bursting suddenly and
    completely
or a breach of a harmonious relationship.

Rupture.

I've forgiven him,
but there's still a collapsed wall
with bricks strewn about.
Our relationship,
broken.

Belong

I hold my stuff
just a little closer.
I don't look at the apartment or the store
or the things I own in the same way.

What's mine?
What belongs to me?
A hairbrush,
three pairs of jeans, all hand-me-downs,
five T-shirts, each one a different color,
three sweaters, a jacket,
all of Ma's old clothes for me to grow into.

I used to have five bobby pins,
then I lost one.
Deep in the drawer of my unfinished pine desk,
a coin purse gifted by my favorite aunt.

Then there's the pinkish-orange sunset
the color of Werner's *love apple,*

a canopy of oak trees,
the wide-open field of St. Augustine grass.

I don't own any of these things,
and yet, they belong to me.

Ahead,
the mountain
and the sheltering sky
don't seem to care
whether I have papers or not.

Today,
the sun shines just as brightly on me,
maybe even more so.

Inside Outside

Shoes are for outside.
Never wear shoes inside the apartment.

Our family, the three of us, are insiders.
Everyone else is an outsider.

They don't want me to tell anyone,
not Tiffany, not the people at church,
no one on the outside,
that our immigration paperwork has expired.

Summer Plans

Now that I have this huge secret,
little things don't seem like such a big deal anymore.

It's toward the end of May,
fewer than three weeks left of school,
and the kids at school are really starting
to talk about summer:
beaches, camps, grandma's house,
vacation to Baja, and TV marathons.

I don't like summer.
If someone asks about my plans,
I'll tell them point-blank,
I'm going to spend the summer working
at my parents' store.

Tiffany's talking about us
sitting out in her backyard
with a bottle of Sun-In.

Uh, what's Sun-In? I ask.

*It's this stuff you spray on
that lightens your hair
when you're out in the sun.*

*Hmm. So it lightens your hair
while you get a tan?*

Yes!

Lightening my hair and getting a tan
are about the last two things
Ma would ever let me do.

Even though she's my best friend,
always, in the back of my mind
when I think about Tiffany
are the words,
inside, outside.

Love Boat

Church kids are talking about summer plans too.

Hey, you going to Love Boat this year?
the older teenagers ask one another.

Love Boat's the nickname for this summer program
where American-born kids
hang out in Taiwan.
They're supposed to be learning
language, history, and culture,
but mostly they do other stuff,
like date each other.

I'm in this weird in-between age,
too old for Vacation Bible School
and not old enough for Love Boat,
which is fine by me.

That way I won't have to explain
why I can't go back to Taiwan.

Making Money

Even before I walk into the store,
I can tell Ma wants to talk.
She's standing by the front counter, waiting.

Hi, Ma!

Ai Shi, I'm going away for the summer.

What? Why?

Mr. and Mrs. Lin called today.
They own a Taiwanese bakery
and asked if I could work for them this summer.
The thing is, their store is in San Diego.

I have so many questions,
but I keep quiet so she can finish talking.
I grab a terry cloth and start wiping the table.

It's too far for me to go back and forth,

so I'll also be staying with them, at their house.
Of course, the only way I can do it
is if you work at the store with Ba.
We'll pay you.

Just then the front door jingles open.
Ma and I both turn our heads at the same time.
It's a customer, someone who looks sort of familiar
but not a regular,
not someone we know by name.

Can I help you? Ma asks,
as she walks toward the counter.

Just like that,
our conversation will have to wait.
It's this unspoken rule we have,
no speaking Mandarin in front of customers.

And for once,
I'm grateful for the interruption.
It gives me time to think of some questions for Ma, like,
Just exactly how much am I going to get paid?

Friends of Friends

Maybe she asked around,
made calls to all the Taiwanese people she knew,
friends and friends of friends.
Maybe she called and told everyone,
Please, we're desperate.
Or maybe the Lins called her on their own,
not knowing that Ma was looking for a summer job.

Either way, by the time I got to the store,
Ma and Ba already talked about
all the money she would make.

Four dollars an hour,
ten hours a day,
seven days a week,
ten weeks of the summer.
4 x 10 x 7 x 10 = $2,800.

That's only $200 shy
of what the lawyer is asking for!

So that's how they decided she would go away,
after they did the math.

Now the only thing left to figure out
is how much I'm going to get paid.

Rich

I wouldn't just be an extra set of hands.
They're counting on me.
Not just to work,
but to *work* work,
to actually, you know, do stuff.
So they should pay me.

I sit there with my arms crossed,
waiting for Ma to say something.
That's the first rule of negotiation:
Don't be the first one to talk.
She's the one who taught me that. Ha!

Ma says,
We'll pay you five dollars a day.

She says a bunch of other things too.
I'm not really listening,
too busy doing math in my head.

Five dollars a day,
Seven days a week,
Ten weeks of the summer,
5 x 7 x 10 = $350!

This is huge, life-changing money.
Brand-new Jordache jeans, Nike shoes,
Hello Kitty backpack, pink Members Only jacket
kind of money!

I don't even wait for Ma to finish talking.

I'll take it!

I guess I'm breaking the second rule of negotiation:
Never take the first offer.
But who cares?
I'm going to be rich!

Funny-Strange

It's been a few days now
and the sheen of all the extra money
is starting to fade, just a little.

Mostly I'm thinking about how
Ma will be gone all summer
and how I'm going to miss her.
I didn't even know she was looking for a summer job.
I only found out after they had already decided.

And it's funny-strange that Ma's going away
to make money,
because business at Dino's
has been pretty good this year.
It's not like the first year,
when we had to dip into savings.
But that's the thing with money,
there can always be more.

Last week, Ba said,

Money makes the world go around.
He said it just like that too, in English,
which makes me think
he didn't come up with it on his own.

Then just yesterday, Ba said,
There are problems even money can't solve.
He said those words in Mandarin.

He's right, I guess.
Our first year here,
we had a problem with break-ins
that money couldn't solve.

Now there's a new problem
money alone can't solve.
But it sure helps.

Summer Job

I've been trying to hold off talking to Tiffany
about my summer job.

I figure I'll tell her when we walk
to Mr. San Filippo's class.
That way, we'll be side by side
and I won't feel her eyes staring at me.

Her jaw drops open.
No way, the whole summer?

Yeah, you can close your mouth now.

Oh my gosh, is that even legal?
I mean, can a kid work at a store all day?
Aren't there laws about this?

Inside, outside.
This is why I don't tell Tiffany stuff sometimes.

Hello, I'm twelve,

and it's not like I work in a sweatshop.
I get breaks.
I get unlimited food and soda,
and for most of the afternoons,
I'll just be sitting there, doing nothing.

Okay, okay, it's just that
I thought we were going to lie out this summer,
you know, work on our tans?

Not really.
Remember I told you
my mom would never let me
lighten my hair or get a tan?

Oh, right.

Besides, aren't you going to Big Bear?

Yeah, but that's just for two weeks.
Are you working the whole summer?
What about the weekends and stuff?

Sorry, Tiff,
not going to happen.

It was never going to happen.

Soon Enough

Ma begins most conversations now with the words,
When I go away.
I wish she didn't do that.
Two weeks will come soon enough.

We try to outdo each other's worry,
as if worrying is just another way to say *I love you.*
She worries I won't have home-cooked food to eat.
I worry she'll get too tired working as a hired hand.

She tells me,
I need you to be strong.
I know when she says *strong* she means not crying.
She hates it when I cry.

Then she asks,
You understand why I'm going away, don't you?

I nod. *Yes, Ma.*

I understand,

but that doesn't make it any easier.

One Hour and Forty-Five Minutes

At school there's a different countdown.
One more week until summer.
While everyone else seems so excited,
I'm going to miss walking
into Mrs. Matthews' classroom
and knowing that in exactly one hour and forty-five
    minutes,
the recess bell will ring.
I'm going to miss knowing what to expect
and what is expected of me.

I'm going to miss my Pee-Chee folders,
the way they keep my papers so neat and tidy.
I'm going to miss doing math homework,
The straight, even lines
of an eight-and-a-half-by-eleven sheet of paper,
the certainty of knowing there is a correct answer,
and the *100%* in red ink Mr. San Filippo writes
on the top right corner of my worksheets.

I'm going to miss school.

Complicated

Mrs. Matthews says,
Every fifty years or so, America redefines what foreign is.

Now she's talking about immigration.
I keep my head down.
Then Mrs. Matthews says,
You know, my great-grandmother was an undocumented
   immigrant.

I look up and stare at blond-haired,
blue-eyed Mrs. Matthews.
She's as American as apple pie and dead serious.

So my great-grandmother wasn't the one
with a ticket to America.
Her sister was.
Right before the ship was to set sail, the sister gets sick.
My great-grandmother takes her spot,
takes her name and identity.
Talk about being undocumented!
I'm telling you this because I want you to know

that immigration stories are complicated.

I look down again,
blinking away tears,
grateful for Mrs. Matthews and her stories.

Trickle Down

Her face is a whole shade lighter,
which makes the freckles on her nose
even more freckly.

Tiff, what's wrong?

My dad lost his job,
and the worst part is,
I can't go to Big Bear Camp this summer.
They want to save money,
so they're sending Trevor and me
to Grandma's house for six weeks.

That's horrible.
I'm really sorry.

I really am sad for Tiffany,
but I'm also secretly a little glad
to know I'm not the only kid
who's affected by adults and their problems

with work and money
that trickle down to us kids.

Under the Table

Only three more days left of school.
I kind of want to talk to Mrs. Matthews
about her great-grandmother,
but mostly I want to avoid talking to Tiffany.

She asks,
But why that job, all the way in San Diego?
She already has a job at the store.
Isn't that enough?
I thought business was actually pretty good.

I don't know, I lie.

Tiffany doesn't really know much about money,
about how it's made
and what people are willing to do
to get more of it.

When Tiffany's dad did go to work,
before he lost his job,
he sat at a desk,

in an air-conditioned office,
while my parents stuck their hands in raw hamburger.

Whenever she says,
I just don't understand,
why does it have to be that job?
I mean, there must be a thousand places she could
work between here and San Diego.

Tiffany doesn't know about the power
of having the right papers.
Mr. and Mrs. Lin are willing to pay Ma in cash,
since she isn't legally allowed to work for other people.
It's called working *under the table.*

I tell her,
I don't know why!
Even though I do know.
And especially I don't want to tell Tiffany
because her dad lost his job,
while Ma has a job working *under the table.*

It's getting harder to lie to Tiffany
because she asks so many questions.
But I want to protect her from the truth,
even though no one is protecting me.

Last Day

I can't be the only kid who's sad
about the last day of school.

I'm going to miss my teachers.
I'm going to miss Mr. San Filippo's lectures
and the cozy feeling in Mrs. Matthews' classroom.

There's still the promotion ceremony tonight,
but since I won't be able to stay and chat afterward,
Tiffany and I say our goodbyes now.
She leaves for Oregon tomorrow.

We're at the school gate.
Her house is to the right,
I have to turn left.

We stand around in silence for two seconds.
I want to ask if we can talk on the phone
but phone calls are expensive,
especially to out of state,
so all I say is,

I hope you have a great time
at your grandma's house!
I'll miss you.

I'll miss you too, she says.
Goodbye.

Ceremony

Ba snaps two photos.
I turn in the polyester cap and gown.

Ba and I walk off the field,
the dwindling sun in the distance.
We move quickly,
because Ma's alone at the store.

I've never been at school
just as twilight gives way to evening,
and everything that's so familiar in the daylight
looks different now.

I see the tree outside Ms. Branch's room,
my constant reading companion last year.
And there, the swings where I spent so much time
wondering about flight and invisibility.
The desert wind is quiet tonight.

Goodbye, Royal Oaks Elementary.
Hello, summer.

Prompt

I empty out my backpack
with its Pee-Chee folders.
Take out two halves of a Pink Pearl eraser,
three paper clips clinging to the front pocket,
a mechanical pencil,
root-beer-flavored ChapStick.

I throw away all the papers,
except for the prompt from Mrs. Matthews,
What America Means to Me.
I set the sheet of paper on top of my desk.

Oranges and Tea

The night before Ma leaves,
the apartment is filled with the scent of oranges
and chrysanthemum.
She takes a sip of tea, clears her throat,
and says, *You know, words are cheap.*

I think to myself,
Maybe that's why she never says
I love you.

Ma keeps talking.
The problem with pretty stories is they're not true.
Stories fill your head with all sorts of ideas,
and then all you're left with is an empty stomach.

I know she's telling me this
because she doesn't want me to read at the store.
She thinks books are a waste of time.
She thinks they're a distraction
from the real world,

and even though she's talking to me,
she's really talking to Ba.
He keeps a book of Tang dynasty poems
hidden next to the soda machine.

I tell her,
Okay, Ma, I won't read at the store.

She nods, takes another sip of tea.
She's done talking.

And I'm left wondering,
Is that it?

Because there's so much more I want her to say.
I want her to tell me she's proud of me,
that she's going to miss me,
that's she's sad to be going away,
that everything will be all right,
yes, especially that everything will be all right,
that she'll come back at the end of summer
and we'll be able to pay the lawyer
and it will be okay.

Any of those things would be better than
words are cheap.

Goodbye

Ba and I drop her off at the Greyhound bus stop.
She wanted it this way.
She's the one who said,
I'll just take the bus to San Diego, because the store.

She has the one big suitcase,
the same one she packed her clothes in from Taiwan.

Ba and I will just leave her there at the bus stop.
We won't even wait with her.
We leave her there with the suitcase
to keep her company.

She said,
Go, go, there's no point in all three of us
waiting for the bus.
I'll see you on the Fourth of July.

It's already been decided.
We'll close the store that day.

It's okay to close the store on a holiday,
especially a holiday when people like to make
their own burgers and ribs at home.

We'll drive down to see her.
And already I'm looking forward
to being in a car for a couple of hours
on the Fourth of July,
to celebrate the holiday like an American.

Two weeks feels like a long time.
I steal sideways glances at Ma
because I don't want to forget anything.
The way she keeps her hair tucked behind her ears,
the way her shoulders slope,
the question mark on her face
when she encounters the outside world.

She kisses Ba on the cheek and me too.

Goodbye, I love you.

I love you too, Ma.

I make it all the way to the car before crying.

Saturday

We get in the Buick
and drive back in time to open the store at eleven.
It's quiet,
nothing unusual,
except for the fact that Ma's not here.
It feels like a Saturday.

Every once in a while,
I remember that Ma's gone
and I tell myself,
It's not so bad,
just like a regular Saturday.

Only it's not.

Ba parks himself by the cash register,
paying attention.
What a weird phrase,
the idea that attention is like money,
something you pay with.

He stands, knees locked,
keys dangling from the chain on his belt,
a slight swayback,
watching,
waiting.

I busy myself with work.
It helps me take my mind off other things,
like our immigration status.

swish, swish,
Jordache jeans

sweep, sweep,
Nike shoes

scrub, scrub,
Members Only jacket.

Sunday

Wooden pews,
a grand piano,
the floor a polished gray slab of concrete.

It's eighty-five degrees out
and Ba is wearing his wool suit.
Sunday is the only day of the week
when he wears old clothes.
His old clothes are his nice clothes.

I like how people at church try so hard,
how we're all dressed up in our finest clothes,
how the stuffy air is a mixture
of drugstore perfume, like Charlie and Wind Song,
with expensive White Shoulders
and Shalimar thrown in.
I like how the adults
sing so loud and off-key
and their bad breath swirls around the room.

They're so eager,
as if they're saying to God,
Look at me. Please, hear me.
And I also say my own silent prayer.

Of course, there are parts of church
I don't like so much.
Like when Pastor Chiang talks about sin,
I can't stop wiggling in my seat,
and I want to tell him, *Stop talking!*

But a part of me understands,
because how else can you explain
all the bad stuff that happens in this world?
What we had to go through last year,
the bullying, the store getting vandalized,
the trouble that glared at us
from a thousand pinprick shards of broken glass,
and then of course this year,
discovering all that was left undone.

I think about the rupture with Ba,
and I don't know why our attempts
to do right and be good fall
so short, even by our own standards.

Monday

The first thing I notice
is what I don't notice.

Silence.

There is no noise coming from the kitchen.
If Ma was here,
there would be the friendly slam of cabinet doors,
the sound of a spoon
stirring against a stainless-steel pot for *muai*,
rice porridge filled with flecks of yellow sweet potato,
next to a plate of thousand-year-old eggs,
pork sung, pickled radishes
and a tin of fish.

Nothing special today,
just Honey Nut Cheerios in a bowl of milk.

Tuesday

Division of labor,
a phrase I learned in school.

Ba works the griddle and the fryer.
I take orders, get the drinks,
and make fried rice.

Before she left, Ma spent days
teaching me how to make fried rice.

Look at how the oil shimmers,
when there's wisps of smoke,
you know it's ready.

Then crumbles of ground pork
already precooked and seasoned with shallots.

This is how you crack an egg with one hand.
Now, use the tip of the metal spatula
to break the yolk.

scramble scramble, salt salt

Bits of celery and green onion.
Try to get both the white and green parts in there.
Now two big ladles of white rice.

salt salt,
stir stir,
fry fry

Ma's family recipe
from all those church potlucks.
At the very end,
something she added all by herself,
something American,
a squeeze of ketchup, Heinz 57.

I make fried rice,
like so many things I do with my hands,
slowly, deliberately.
I say a quick prayer as I work,
Please, God, let everything be okay.
Let the summer pass quickly.

Wednesday

Sometimes I forget.
It's as if nothing bad has happened
and everything is just like before.

Ba, my first friend.

Today the supplier delivered a box of Popsicles.
We'll sell them for twenty-five cents each.
Ba tells me that for every five Popsicles we sell,
I can eat one.
We'll probably sell five a day.

I spend the afternoon staring
at the wide open stretch of Route 66.
I think about the speech prompt,
What America Means to Me.

Thursday

What summer is not:
Star Trek TV marathon,
swimming at the beach,
the ice cream truck,
thin discs of Pringles
stacked perfectly,
unbroken.

Instead, summer is:
hot kitchen,
sizzle of beef fat,
buzz of fluorescent lights,
two refrigerators that stand like sentries.

The day is long and lean
and there is no language
in the quiet of the afternoon.

Only occasional
one-syllable words:

hi
large Coke
fries
to go
thank you

The cash register's electronic beep,
tinkling coins,
hissing soda dispenser,
splash of frozen fries belly flopping
into a vat of frying grease,
lying limp in a pool of oil,
then, gurgling, gurgling,
they swim to the surface.

Five minutes.

The pitter-patter of feet,
metal clanging against metal,
drip, drip, drip of oil,
crinkling paper bag.

Smile.

The handoff deserves a complete sentence:
Here are your fries.

Thank you.

You're welcome.

Goodbye.

Friday

Day seven,
feels more like twenty-seven.

The bank at 9:30,
the store by 10:00,
work,
no reading,
closing time at 8:30,
home by 8:37,
watch TV,
take a shower,
sleep,
repeat.

Saturday

The different kinds of boring.
There's the kind that other kids complain about,
in that singsong voice,
Mom, I'm bored,
and then they get a snack
and turn on the TV.

I'm talking about the kind of boredom
that chips away,
tick, tick, tick
of the clock on the back wall,
the taste of metal,
a headache.

Boredom is the fallow ground
where half-finished thoughts
never make it across the finish line.

But then I realize,
Today is payday!

And nothing is more exciting than money!
Ba hands over thirty-five dollars.

It's been exactly one week since Ma left.

Outsider

On our way to church,
Ba starts to talk like the way he used to talk,
to pass the time.
Only now, he's telling stories
about his *lao jia*, where he's from,
stories he's never told before.

I was about your age
when I went away for school
to continue my education.
The small village I lived in had nothing
beyond elementary school.
So, I had to go away.

I didn't go too far,
just the next town.
It was far enough that I had to leave home
and live away from my family
for weeks at a time.

I was grateful that your zu fu
was willing to pay for my schooling.
But it was also a difficult time,
my first experience of being an outsider.

I don't want you to think
I had an unhappy childhood.
I always knew my parents loved me.

That's the one thing
I hope you know.
No matter what happens,
know that your mother and I,
we love you.

Ba and I sit
in the silence of his lingering words,
traveling westward in the Buick,
the mountain in the distance.

Brick by brick,
the wall is being repaired.

Day of Rest

We leave church right away after the service.
We haven't yet figured out how to tell people
that Ma's gone for the summer.

This is our half day off
and we want to make the most of it
before we open the store at four.
Ba drives to the thrift shop,
the one between Pasadena and Duarte.
We head straight to the back,
past the glass display cases of beads and baubles,
past the old-lady employees in their baby-blue smocks.

There are shelves of *National Geographic*s,
a set of *World Encyclopedia*s,
stacks of *Choose Your Own Adventure* books.

Ba says,
Pick out a book.
It's the Sabbath, a day of rest.

You can read today.

I want to so bad,
but then I remember the promise I made to Ma
about not reading at the store.
I'm confused because Ba's saying,
It's the Sabbath, you can read,
even though that would mean breaking the promise
I made to Ma.
And we're not even supposed to work on the Sabbath.

In the end, I grab two books.
One called *Bridge to Terabithia*,
which I picked because of the cover,
and another book, *The Outsiders*.
That one I chose because of the title.

Short and Sweet

Three o'clock Sunday afternoon,
the phone call begins with Ba saying,
yi qian yi bai,
one thousand one hundred,
how much the store made this past week.
It's not uncommon for Ma and Ba
to greet each other with a number after saying hello.

Ma tells us about Mr. and Mrs. Lin's bakery,
how they treat her well,
how she's not too tired,
how she can smell the ocean
from their house in San Diego.

Then she asks if I've been *guai.*
Guai is this word that means equal parts
obedient and good.

I say, *Yes,*
even as I remember all the ways

I haven't been so obedient.

She tells me she's proud of me
and that she's lucky to have such a wonderful daughter.

Everything is *good* and *okay*
because more than anything else,
phone calls are about saying positive things
so the other person doesn't feel bad.
That's why, even if it was the case,
Ma would never say *my back hurts*
or *it's hard being on my feet all day.*

Besides, even calls within California are expensive.
We have to pay by the minute.
That's another reason to keep the conversation
short and sweet.

Not Here

I think what I love most
about reading
is how
I can be here
and also,
not here.

Terabithia,
Tulsa,
anywhere but here.

First

Monday morning, Ba says,
Ma's not here, and it's not fair
that she gets to make all the rules.
How about if we let some of her rules slide?

Like what?

Well, let's work backwards.
Instead of just blindly following rules,
what are the principles we want to live by?

Ba loves talking about principles.

He says, *Well, I think the first principle should be,*
"Treat the customers right."

Uh, I think the phrase is,
"The customer is always right."

I know I'm changing it.

I don't believe the customer is always right.
And there's that other American saying,
"The customer is king."
If I treated the customer like a king,
then there go all my profits.
But I believe that if you treat people with respect,
they will do the same to you.

So that's how he came up with the first principle.
I have to sit at the front of the store at all times,
keep an eye out for customers.
And when a customer does walk in,
I have to smile and say right away,
Hello, welcome to Dino's!
How can I help you?

Second

The second principle is:
Pace yourself.
Be aware of how much energy you have.

So that's why Ba always starts the day off moving slowly.
In the mornings, he takes his time
lifting heavy boxes of lettuce, onions, and tomatoes.
He moves slowly,
almost like he's doing tai chi.
He's trying to save his energy,
because he has to work another ten hours.

At the end of the night though,
Ba has all this extra energy
because it'll be time to go home soon.

The other thing that gives Ba energy is counting money.
Right before closing, he does the final count
of how much money the store has made that day.
He puts the twenties in his pocket

for us to take to the bank the next morning.

He empties out the cash register

of all the coins and bills

and places the money

in a small canvas bag,

exactly like the kind you'd see in a cartoon.

Third

The third principle is a combination of little rules
that are mostly about what
you should and shouldn't do in front of customers.
I call it the *be clean and look nice* principle.

No touching your face or hair.
No eating in front of customers.
Keep your fingernails short and clean.
Always smile,
even when you don't feel like it.

Fourth

The fourth principle:
Anything that does not violate
the above three principles is allowed.

Tai chi is allowed,
because it helps with managing one's energy.
It must be done in the back of the store, of course,
behind the refrigerators, where customers can't see.

Drinking soda is always allowed
because soda puts you in a good mood
and helps keep away daytime sleepiness.

This principle is how we decided,
once and for all,
that reading at the store is allowed.

Your mother thinks reading is a distraction from work,
but reading helps with managing one's energy.
I think reading should be allowed

as long as it doesn't violate any of the other principles.
You just have to put the book down
the moment a customer walks into the store.

So even though I'd promised Ma
I wouldn't read at the store,
I start reading every day of the week
and not just on Sundays.

I'm not doing anything wrong or hurting anyone,
and besides, reading keeps my mind
off the *what ifs* and the *if onlys*
that want to take root in my head like:
What if some other bad thing happens?
What if our new visa application is rejected?
What if we'll always be right outside the promised land,
watching, waiting, and never able to enter?

Dove's Eyes

After I broke the promise about reading in the store,
it wasn't too hard to break the other promise,
the one about not hiding in the bathroom.

Only I don't go in there to get out of work.
I go to splash water on my face,
make sure my hair is parted nicely to the side.

I put the toilet seat lid down and sit,
just for a minute.
The bathroom is clean and quiet,
and it's a place for me to be alone with my thoughts.

Then I look in the mirror
until I no longer
recognize the person staring back.

I look at the girl,
who looks like me
but is not me.

I look into her dove eyes
until I hear her say,
Everything's going to be okay.

Catch the Wind

What about roller skating? Is that allowed?

Ba takes off his reading glasses,
as if he's really thinking hard, and says,
*Yes, because roller skating is exercise
and exercise helps manage energy.*

So right before the dinner rush,
after the sun is a little lower in the sky
but the ground is still so hot
I can see waves of air tumbling over the asphalt,
I skate round and round
the parking lot,
while Ba keeps watch over the store.

I turn,
catch the desert wind,
and for a moment
I feel as though
I'm cutting through air,
flying.

Intention

In the afternoons
Ba and I inhabit two separate worlds
built by the scaffolding of words.
His world is in Chinese.
Mine is in English,
and there's a divide.

He's happy to see me reading a book,
but he's sad about the trade-off.
The more I love English,
the faster my gradual unlearning of Chinese.

So Ba adds one final rule:
Chinese School is allowed,
because you must never forget Chinese.

One hour every afternoon, he becomes my teacher.
He takes a used order sheet,
a piece of paper with
hamburger, fries, x-large Coke

scribbled on the front,
flips it over,
and writes the word for horse, 馬,
a word I've seen hundreds of times.

Today I see something else,
four galloping legs,
the swish of a tail.
I see intention,
Ba's love for language,
and the beauty of the written word.

Blue

It's going to be different this week.
The Fourth of July falls on a Sunday.
The good news is we only lose
half a day of business instead of a whole day.
The bad news is I don't get paid when I don't work.
The coming week's paycheck will only be thirty dollars.

We're in the Buick, heading south to see Ma.
I'm a little nervous.
We only have this one day together,
and I've missed her.

The highway turns.
In the near distance,
water.

The sky and water in conversation,
blue echoing blue.

It's just as I remember,

and *Werner's Nomenclature of Colours*
cannot capture the swirling ocean of
azure,
cerulean,
ultramarine,
celadon,
and the blue of my memory.

I used to swim in this ocean,
the Pacific,
on the other side of the world.

Ba says,
We'll pick her up
and come back here.
It'll be just like old times.

I look out the window.
The smell of salt water,
the boundless sea,
the three of us.

Facing the Water

We buy shorts, swimsuits,
hats, and sunscreen.
We buy as if we're cramming
a year's worth of vacation into a day.

We sit on the sand
and let the color of the ocean wash over us.

Only then do we talk.
How have you been? Ma asks.
Our faces are turned away from each other,
towards the water.

Good. I've been good, I say.

I ask her what it's like
to work for other people.

She says, *It's fine.*
I'm learning a lot from them

about how to run a business.

I can tell she's holding back.
She's not telling me everything
because she doesn't want me to worry.

I don't want her to worry either.
I tell her about my speech
and all the writing I've done on
What America Means to Me.

She's listening, really listening
as we sit facing the water,
the endless shining sea.

Wave

Ba is the first one to get up.
He walks to the water,
his back straight,
as if he's walking towards an old friend.
He dips into the ocean.
We don't see him again until moments later
when a wave carries him back to us.

His body crumpled,
arms splayed,
laughing.

And even still
I'm shy,
uncertain.

I walk to the edge
and keep walking.
The waves sweep over me.

Lost, and then found.

Rearview Mirror

We drop Ma off
and begin the two-hour drive back.

Dusk settles around the car,
as the sky fades into darkness.

I didn't know how much I needed today,
to not work,
to not be at the store,
to be tired in an entirely different way,
to smell the ocean
and now to be in a car, moving
with the blur of twinkling lights around me.

Anna?

He hardly ever calls me by my American name.
I look up to see his eyes in the rearview mirror.

I want you to live a big life.
Don't be like me.

I've lived a small life.

I look at the night sky.
I trace the faint outline of stars.

Do you know what I mean by a big life?
I want you to dream big dreams
and work hard
and be happy.
I know there are
obstacles you have to overcome.

He falters, stops talking.
A moment later, he starts again.

You can be anything you want.
You can do anything.
Promise me you'll try, Annie.

He's looking at me through the rearview mirror.

Okay, Ba.
I promise.

Brick by Brick

And even though the days are the same,
each day is also a little different:
a story about Ba's *lao jia*,
a detail about *zu mu*, my father's mother,
a special lesson during Chinese School.

The only sad part is I miss Ma.
But even the sadness of missing her is not so sad,
because missing Ma is mixed up
with being grateful for her.
Sometimes sadness is a part of love.

Gone

Just exactly how long is a moment?
Most people don't know this.
I looked it up in the dictionary.
A moment is a fixed amount of time,
ninety seconds.

Isn't that funny?
I thought a moment was much shorter,
almost like something that's already gone,
once you take notice.
By the time you say to yourself,
Here it is,
this is a moment,
it's already no longer here.

And now, boredom
has almost become an old friend.
When I sense that she is nearby,
I turn to look at her
and she's gone.

In Between

I don't want to rush through these days
of swimming in poetry.
We're reading through all of Li Bai's poems.
I've committed to memory
my own translation of "Long Yearning."

The sky is long, the road is far,
bitter in between, my sorrow.
In a dream,
I cannot reach the mountain.
Yearning
cuts through my heart.

I'm starting to write my own poems.

Ming 明

Two words,
the sun, 日,
and the moon, 月,
together
is *ming*, 明,
meaning clear,
bright,
shining.

Clear and bright
is the light
of the sun and the moon.

Sky is *tian*, 天,
a line with a big person, 大,
underneath.

Ming tian, 明 天,
is the passing of one sun 日
and one moon 月
in the sky 天.

Ming tian, 明 天, tomorrow.

Return

I crane my head to look at the store
when we pass.

Almost always, for a moment,
I forget to breathe.
Bad habit, I guess.

Then I see her,
a girl with sun-bleached red hair
and floppy sandals
sitting under a sliver of shade.

It's Tiffany!
She's back from her grandma's.

Between Lunch and Dinner

She comes by the next day
and then again a few days after that.
Just in the afternoons
for a couple of hours
between lunch and dinner,
when time slows down.

Tiffany helps me with the sweeping and mopping.
I give her an orange Fanta Dew.
We sit at the corner table,
munching on fries.

Ba offers to make her some real food.
He says it's the least he can do
after all the spaghetti dinners I've had at her house.
But Tiffany says,
Naw, I'm good with fries, Mr. Zhang.

I toss her an Otter Pop
as she's leaving.

How's your dad? I ask.

He's the same.
He says he's looking for a job.
All I see him do is play Atari.

Sorted Out

There is no reason to be nervous,
but I am,
nervous about Ma coming home in a week.

Of course, I've missed her.
And when she comes back,
we'll go see the lawyer.
Our immigration status will get sorted out,
and every thing will be ok.

So why am I nervous?

End of Summer

There's one more thing.
Maybe it's that Ma coming back
means the end of summer.
And now that summer is almost over,
I don't want it to end.

It hasn't been so bad,
not nearly half as bad
as I thought it'd be.

And who knows,
maybe one day,
I'll look back on this summer
and miss the moments I spent
talking about poetry with Ba
and miss all the time I spent wishing
I was anywhere but here.

Maybe someday,
I'll look for a way back.
Maybe words will be my way back.

Seen

We could have gone to pick her up
and made it back in time
to open the store on a Sunday,
but she said,
Save the gas money.
I'll take the bus.

Now I'm sitting at the counter,
looking for RTD bus number 287.

My eyes trail the passing of cars
moving from one side of the street to the other,
as if I'm tracking a tennis match in slow motion.

A bus stops in front of the store.
I watch and wait.
There's Ma,
one foot after the other,
stepping off the bus
with her luggage in tow.

I'm surprised at how small she looks.
Her hair is pinned back with jet-black bobby pins,
a hint of red lipstick sets off the rest of her face.

I keep looking at her,
aware that I only have a few more seconds
before her eyes adjust
and she'll see me through the glare of glass.
I wait, watching for that moment of recognition.

Her eyes crinkle just a bit.
She sees me.
Her face brightens into a smile.

Tres Leches

She wants to open the refrigerator doors
and examine the freshness of the coleslaw.
She wants to look at the size of the hamburger patties
and test the quality of the oil.

We make her sit in the back.
No working, we tell her.
You should rest.

We use Ma's homecoming as an excuse
to close ten minutes early.
We turn off the lights and rush out
of the store like bandits,
before a lone customer saunters in to halt our getaway.

It's only after we're safely in the car that Ba asks,
What do you want for dinner?
The Chinese place or the taco stand?

Ma scrunches up her nose and says,

I'd rather have good Mexican food
than bad Chinese food any day!

We drive down Route 66
for menudo and tacos al pastor,
our plates filled with lime wedges, radishes,
pickled jalapeños, and cilantro.
A string of lights around the restaurant
glow in celebration.

Then, just as we finish our meal,
the owner brings over a wedge of cake.
Gratis, he says.
A slice of cake, on the house.
It's called tres leches,
made from honey
and three different kinds of milk.

We each take a small bite.
Ba orders two more slices
so everyone has their own.

Night has completed its descent.
Still we linger at the restaurant.
I eat my cake slowly, savoring
the taste of milk and honey in the promised land.

Twenty-Eight

I unpack her suitcase,
lug the dirty clothes down the stone walkway,
and start a load of laundry.
I massage her feet.

Ba brews chrysanthemum tea.
We turn on every lamp in the apartment,
flooding the place with light.

Ba and I take turns counting the money.
When it's my turn,
I take the wad of hundred-dollar bills into my left hand,
use my thumb to feed each bill
into the receiving fingers of my right,
counting with each flick,
one, two, three.

The crisp snap of cash,
the blur of green flashing before my eyes,
Benjamin Franklin's big chin

bobbing up and down with each swipe.
Twenty-eight, add two zeroes to make
two thousand eight hundred dollars.

I dip my toe in happiness.

Cost

Only after the money is counted and put away
does Ma begin to talk.
Mr. and Mrs. Lin were very kind to me.
It was a good learning experience,
but I wouldn't want to do it again.
I'd much rather work at my own store
and be at home with you two.

She falls silent and then, a little later,
she says,
It's all been worth it, though.
It's part of the cost of immigrating
that the first generation pays.
But I know, Ai Shi, you have also had to pay.

What do you mean? I ask.

You've had to sacrifice too, Ai Shi.
I see what you had to give up.
Thank you for working this summer.

That's okay, I say,
and then after a moment, *You're welcome.*

She's had these words all along.
She was just waiting for the right time.

Law Office

We dress up in our nicest Sunday clothes
even though it's Tuesday.
We close the store today.

210 to 110
then 10
to downtown LA,
the lawyer's office.

Fancy plaques on the wall,
leather-bound volumes of books
that look like a matching set of encyclopedias.
A marble table, brass lamps,
the smell of stale paper.

The lawyer is wearing a cream-colored silk blouse
against the black backdrop of a pantsuit.
Her hair is set in soft, bouncy curls.
In another life,
Ma could have been mistaken for this woman's sister,

but here in this wood-paneled office,
the silk-blouse lawyer
looks more like Harvard Law than Ma.

Ma and Ba tell her our story,
down to the kitchen cabinet stuffed full of mail.
After two minutes the silk-blouse lawyer
decides she's heard enough.
She takes a deep breath and starts talking,
cuts Ba off mid-sentence.
I need you to understand,
by applying to renew your I-94 status,
you are drawing attention to the fact
that you're already currently fei fa.

Ma and Ba have always used the term *yi min shen fen*
when talking about our immigration status.
Now the lawyer is using a phrase
I haven't heard before,
fei fa.
I understand the words separately,
fa is *law,*
fei is the prefix *no,*
as in *no law,*
not legal,
illegal.

Again and Again

Now it's his turn to cut her off.
What are our options? Ba asks.

The lawyer takes a deep breath and says,
The Immigration and Naturalization Service
may approve a new I-94
or they may deny you.
That's the gamble you're taking when you apply.
You're drawing attention to the fact
that you're already fei fa.
If they deny you, then they may deport you.
Now, they're not actively deporting people right now,
but you'll be on their radar.

Wait, so what are you suggesting? Ma asks.

The lawyer replies,
I'm not advising that you break the law,
but you don't have to do anything, she says,
waving her hand with a flick of the wrist.

It's actually quite common.
People get confused by the different dates
on the I-94 and the E-2 all the time
and that's how they get in trouble.
Just remember, the E-2 is a visa
which allows for legal entry into a country,
and the I-94 is a document that dictates
the visa holder's length of stay.
But even if they approve a new visa for you,
you'll be in the same situation in another year.
You'll need to apply again and again,
so on and so forth.
You will not be any closer to traveling
on the path to citizenship.
You know that, right?

Ma and Ba look at each other.
Their heads bob up and down in unison.
I hold my head perfectly still.
I didn't know any of this.

Path to Citizenship

Excuse me? I ask.
The lawyer stops talking, turns her head
to give me her full attention.

I know what I'm doing is very rude,
interrupting adults when they're talking
about important stuff.
Well, I just found out I'm *illegal*.
I think I can be a little rude.

The lawyer tilts her chin,
permitting me to speak.

*What do you mean we're
not going to be any closer on the path to citizenship?
Isn't that what we're paying you for,
to get our papers in order
so we can apply for citizenship?* I ask.

Ma tries to shush me,

But the lawyer gives a small chuckle
as if she's amused.

The kind of visa your family has, the E-2,
was never going to get you citizenship.
The E-2 allows you to live and work alongside Americans,
but you'll never become an American
through that route.
The E-2 must be renewed every few years,
and if you ever stop renewing,
then you lose the legal right to stay.
To get citizenship, you have to find another path.

So what are these other paths? I ask.

The lawyer replies,
You can get a rich relative to sponsor you,
or if you get a job at a fancy company,
they may be willing to apply on your behalf.
Or if you're a genius,
you might be able to get an Einstein Visa.
But if you're hoping to apply
through the regular lottery system,
the chances are very slim.

Now I know why Ma and Ba were nodding their heads.
They've known this all along.

I close my eyes.
The three of them keep talking,
back and forth.

I stopped listening when the lawyer said,
You can apply and risk deportation
or not apply and risk deportation.
What do you want to do?

Chance

Last year a kid called me Chinaman,
so I looked up the word
in the dictionary,
because it sounded wrong,
but I didn't know why.

The dictionary definition:
Chinaman,
a term used to refer
to a Chinese person,
offensive.

My eyes lingered on the page,
and underneath was another entry:
Chinaman's chance,
an extremely slim chance,
a hopeless undertaking.

No one really knows the origin of its usage.
It began popping up in American newspapers in 1893.

Some suspect that the phrase is in reference to the fact
that the American legal system in the 1800s
almost always
ruled against the Chinese.

Whenever I hear someone talking about *chance*,
I hear the words, *Chinaman's chance*.
I can't help it.

Pinball

The car ride back
from downtown LA,
traffic is so bad,
one minute we're careening at sixty-five miles per hour.
In a split second,
Ba slams on the brakes to a screeching halt.

Dr. Elisabeth Kübler-Ross was wrong
about how one passes through
the five stages of grief
in an orderly way.

No, the stages of grief are random,
like a steel ball ricocheting
in a pinball machine.

The ball slams
from denial to bargaining to anger.
ding! ding! ding!

No rhyme or reason,
only velocity
and rage.

Look, Seek, Ask

It's quiet.
I spend the next few days
watching and waiting.

What now?
Will they look into selling the store and moving back?
Will we just figure it out as we go along
and hope for the best?
Will they ask me how I'm feeling?

Nothing.

Gravity

I slice through the middle of a cabbage.
The knife slips,
falls.

I lunge for it.

Ma yells,
No, never try to catch a falling knife!

Why?

You could cut your hand.
You wait for the knife to hit the ground,
then pick it up.

But what if I can catch it?

You already lost control
when the knife left your hand.
You can't fight gravity.

Just let the law of nature take its course.

Now I know she's not just talking about the knife.
I can tell, they're not going to look for another lawyer.
They're just going to do exactly
what the silk-blouse lawyer said,
which was, *do nothing.*

I stand still,
listen for the sound
of a knife hitting the ground.

I don't hear a thing.

Less Than

Sometimes math helps me understand.

Inequalities are expressed
by the terms *less than, greater than, equal to.*

If I had to guess what my parents are thinking
as an inequality,
it would look like this:
being illegal in the promised land
is greater than
being a citizen elsewhere.

Or this:
living in a country with fair and free elections
even when you can't vote
is greater than
voting in a country without fair and free elections.

And this one's my favorite:
the hope of one day being a citizen in the promised land

is greater than
the current reality of being illegal.

Third Name

Ai Shi,
Anna,
Today I settle into my new name, *Illegal*.

I say the word,
feel it on my tongue,
let it pull and stretch in my mouth.

Illegal, Illllleeeegal

I say it over and over again,
Illegal, Illegal, Illegal.

I try to render it meaningless through repetition.
Still, it stings.

Syllogisms

The parade of thoughts
as I sit on a wooden pew at church.

God is love.
God hates sin.
Being illegal is breaking the law.
Breaking the law is a sin.
I am a sinner.
Does God hate me?

I don't know which of these is true.

Lord's Prayer

When it's time to pray
with everyone else, I say,

Father in heaven,
You are holy,
        and I am not.

Your kingdom come,
Your will be done
on earth as it is in heaven.
        Was it your will for us to become illegal?

Give us this day our daily bread,
        or a bowl of rice.

Forgive us our trespasses,
        I am nothing if not a trespasser.

Just as we forgive those who have trespassed against us.
        There are so many.

Lead us not into temptation,
>I will continue to trespass, God.
>That is who I am.

But deliver us from the evil one
>for nothing can separate us from your love.

Amen.

Levi's Jeans

This isn't how I pictured it.
I spent all summer working and saving.
Here I am, in old Levi's
and dirty sneakers
on the first day of school.

I don't feel anything,
not happy,
not sad,
just blah.

Is this the stage of grief
Dr. Kübler-Ross calls depression?

Werner's Sulfur Yellow

Junior high's different from elementary school.
Some of the girls wear makeup,
like Heather McPherson, who lines her eyes in blue,
which is funny, because just a few months ago
she was still playing Hungry Hungry Hippos.

Ma would never let me wear makeup,
and Mrs. Nagel's the same way with Tiffany.
Neither of us have gone back-to-school shopping at all.
I'd rather just hold on to my money,
and Tiffany can't go,
because her dad still hasn't found a job.
So the two of us are still hanging out in our old clothes.

Until today.
Tiffany shows up in this outfit from Gemco.
I know because I saw those clothes
featured in last week's mailer.
Head to toe, paisley and penny loafers.

You went shopping? I ask.

Yes, do you like it?

Sure! But I thought your mom wanted to save money.

Oh, my dad finally got a job.
He found out on Friday
and Mom took me shopping on Saturday.

That's nice, I say,
zipping up my jacket to cover up
a dingy yellow shirt.

Bad Joke

The Speech Club prompt sits on my pine desk
like a taunt until I call its bluff.
I crumple up the sheet of paper into a ball.

I don't want to join the Speech Club.
I don't want to be a lawyer anymore.

Because the law doesn't care
how much you want to be an American.
The law doesn't care that you cry
when the music teacher plays
that dumb Woody Guthrie song,
"This Land Is Your Land."
The law doesn't reward you for coming forward.
Instead, it wants the undocumented to keep hiding.

Besides, how can I talk about being a lawyer
when I've broken the law,
when I'm *an illegal*?

Because now it just sounds like
the beginning of a bad joke:
What do you call the illegal
who wants to be a lawyer?

An oxymoron.
That's me, the punch line.

Empty Stomach

What's this?
Isn't this for the speech you're working on?

Ba points to the papers I threw in the trash.

I've stopped working on it, I tell him.

Why, Annie?

Because words don't make a difference.
It's like what Ma used to say.
"Words fill your head with pretty stories
only to leave you with an empty stomach."

I'm sorry you think that way,
but it's not true.
If we don't have hope,
what do we have, Ai Shi?

Nothing.

I walk out of the room
without saying a word.
Why answer with words
when my whole point is that words don't matter?

What You Need

I'll just work at the store when I grow up.
Of course, it's not what they want,
working with my hands.
I don't think I have a lot of choices.
It's like that Rolling Stones song,
"You Can't Always Get What You Want."

Besides, there is nothing wrong
with cooking food for a living.
If I don't draw any attention to myself,
the INS won't come to look for me.
It'll be nice and quiet,
hiding behind these two refrigerators,
an okay life.

I used to think I would be all right
as long as I had my books.
But I haven't picked up a book
since that day at the lawyer's office.

I haven't read a story,
or thought of a poem
or cracked open the dictionary.

It hurts too much.

Lunchtime

Clubs start meeting the second week of school,
during lunchtime.
Before Tiffany left for the summer
I had convinced
her to join Speech Club too.

We're right outside Mr. Hernandez's classroom.
Tiffany's about to walk in.
I'm a half step behind her
when I say,
You go ahead.
I just realized I have some homework to do.

Right now?

Yeah, I have to go to the library to finish my algebra.
Better hurry, the meeting's about to start.

Then I walk away,
past Building D, and enter the library

through the back entrance.
I know I'm being super rude to Tiff,
not telling her that I changed my mind
about the Speech Club,
but being rude is the least of my worries.
I spend the rest of lunch working on my algebra,
even though the homework's not due for
another two days.

Crossing the Border

They're going to Tijuana this Saturday.
It's like all the sadness of Mr. Nagel losing his job
has gone out the window
and everything is the way it was before.
Tiffany asks if I want to tag along.

Tijuana's in Mexico.
There is no way I can cross the border.

I can't.
My parents need me at the store, I say.

Can't you just tell them you're taking the day off?

No, I can't.

Sometimes I think you use the store as an excuse,
Tiffany says.

You don't know what it's like.
The worst thing that's ever happened to you
is your dad losing his job.
All you lost out on was Big Bear Lake.

Hey, look Anna,
I'm not interested in having a comparison contest
about who's had it worse, okay?
Now do you want to go to Tijuana with my family or not?

Nope, sorry Tiff.
I gotta work.

I don't think I'll ever be able
to tell her the truth.

Freeloading

Am I just especially sensitive,
or is there extra chatter these days about illegals?

On KTLA's nightly news,
a man speaks into a reporter's microphone, saying,
I'm sick and tired of illegals taking our jobs.
I'm sick and tired of illegals freeloading
and not paying into the system.

He's not saying anything I haven't heard before.
Mostly, I'm curious about this man
and why he's so afraid of losing his job to illegals.
I want to know if he works
in the kitchen of a restaurant,
or cleans houses,
or babysits children,
or washes cars,
or pushes a lawn mower,
or picks fruit,
or gives manicures,

or plucks chickens,
or maybe he works somewhere, anywhere,
under the table,
and that's why he's so afraid
of illegals taking his job.

But if I had to guess,
I bet this guy works
in a place with air-conditioning.
I bet he sits at a desk,
and drinks free coffee.
I bet he gets sick time,
vacation time, and holidays off.
I bet he gets health insurance
and, if he's lucky, dental insurance too.

The man talks about how he's not against immigration.
He says, *They just have to do it legally.*
They need to get in line like everyone else.

I've heard this before too
and it sounds good.
I mean, who can argue with that?
Even a four-year-old knows
how to stand in line.

But it's not just one line.
There are many separate lines
depending on the applicant's country of origin.
And people from certain countries
wait much longer.
People wait years and years,
and still,
some never make it.

Ma and Ba came here for a better life,
and I tagged along because I was just a kid
who didn't know any better.
But we've made a life here,
and we want to stay.

We don't take up much space
in our little corner of the desert,
right outside the promised land.

Science Class

Symbiosis is the close ecological relationship
of two different species.

And within symbiosis,
the relationships are even further defined:
parasitism,
commensalism,
and *mutualism*.

Parasitism is when one organism
benefits at the expense of another.
The parasite lives on or in the body of the host,
causing harm and possibly even death.

That guy being interviewed on KTLA's nightly news,
he would probably say that illegals
and America have a parasitic relationship.
He's wrong.

A much better illustration is commensalism,

where one species benefits
and the other is completely unaffected,
like an orchid growing on a tree branch.
Or even better, there's mutualism.
Consider clown fish and anemone.
Anemone provide shelter,
while clown fish provide nutrients.
Mutualism is a relationship in which
both parties benefit.

Choice

The speech prompt handout,
rescued from the trash
and smoothed of its creases,
is laid out on my desk.

I stomp into the living room,
waving the sheet of paper in my hand.
What is this?

It's the Speech Club prompt, Ba replies.

I know, I threw it in the trash.
Why did you fish it out?

I thought you should reconsider.
I think you'd really enjoy being part of the Speech Club.

I already told you.
Words don't make a difference.
Words can't change anything.

What do you mean?

Our situation.
We're illegal and no dumb speech
is going to change that.
So why should I bother?

You should bother because you love words.
We're undocumented.
That's our status right now,
but that doesn't completely define you.
Ultimately, you choose who you become.

Oh really?
What can I choose to be?

You can choose to be the beloved daughter
of Zhang Ai Han and Wang Chu Chen.

You can choose to be a writer,
a student of the word.

You can choose to love the world,
this world that God created.

You have so many choices, Ai Shi.
You get to decide.

A Long Moment

I summon up
all the courage I have,
which is not very much.

Ma?

Yes?

What are we going to do?

I know
she knows what I mean.
Her jaw tightens for just a moment,
and she begins to speak slowly, softly.
You heard the lawyer,
we're not going to . . .

Before she can finish,
even as my mouth is clenched shut,
I silently scream,
No!

I run
out the back door.

I fall,
tumbling
onto the asphalt,
this land that we own,
this land that does not belong to us.

The back door creaks open.

How long have I been out here?
Long enough for tears to dry
and stain my face twice over.

Ma sits down.
She waits as I say
the one fully formed sentence
that's been rattling in my head
on repeat,
I don't know how we're supposed to live.

Ma holds me close.
It's so quiet
I can hear the sound
of her heartbeat.

And after a long moment,
my heart is beating in unison with hers.

Only then does she answer.
We wait
and while we wait,
we live.

Live

Ma hands me a hundred dollars
and says, *Go buy some new clothes.*
It's a little late to go back-to-school shopping,
but better late than never.

I take the cash.
That's one of the rules about money,
Always take cash when it's offered.
Then I ask,
Why? I have my own money.

Ma replies,
I can give my daughter money if I want.
I have an extra $2,800, remember?

I do remember.
They never did have to pay the lawyer.

She tells me,
We shouldn't be so busy surviving

that we forget to live.
Go be a regular kid today.

Break

Late September,
the sun gives us a break from its constant stare
and the land cools, just a bit.

Tiffany and I are on our way to Santa Anita Mall.
I never thought I'd miss the lurching,
the constant starting and stopping of the bus.

We plan out our day,
stores like the Gap, Contempo Casuals,
and Spencer's Gifts.
Lunch at Hot Dog on a Stick
and afterwards, Waldenbooks.

It's going to be a good day, I tell myself,
even as a little knob of worry
flits back and forth in my stomach.

Hey, Tiff?

Yeah?

I'm sorry I've been such a bad friend.
Tiffany's quiet, so I keep talking.
Like when I left you in the lurch about Speech Club.

Oh that. It's all right.
But you have seemed kind of distracted lately.

Remember when I said I couldn't go
with your family to Tijuana?

Yeah?

The reason I couldn't go is because
my immigration paperwork is out of whack.

Oh, so you can't leave the country
or something?

Right, I can't.

But what about visiting your relatives
in Taiwan?

I can't do that either,

not until our immigration status is figured out.

I'm sorry, that sucks.

Yeah, it does.
Do you have any other questions for me?

Not really.
Oh, can we get some Orange Julius?

Yes, let's do it!

Born to Run

Kids are munching on chips
and drinking from pouches of Capri Sun.

We tiptoe,
try to make ourselves small
as we make our way to the back.

There's a huge American flag jutting out from the wall
and posters plastered all over the room:
a portrait of Martin Luther King Jr.,
a man with X for a last name,
a sign that reads, *Boycott Grapes,*
Bruce Springsteen's *Born to Run* album cover,
and a picture of a woman, Dorothy Day,
next to the quote,
Love in action is a harsh and dreadful thing,
compared with love in dreams.

I read these words
and think about Ma and Ba,

how they've had to do some
harsh and dreadful and beautiful things.

From the corner, a voice cries out,
It's nice to see some new faces today.
Welcome to Speech Club.
I'm Mr. Hernandez!

Sorry, We're Closed

I tell them,
It's important to me
that both of you are there
for my speech.

They look at each other.
Then Ba says,
Sure, sure, we can close the store for an hour.
Help me make a sign to put on the door.

I write in my best handwriting,
Gone fishing, be back by 2!

Waiting

The multipurpose room is packed.
Ma and Ba are in the audience
to hear me speak
about America,
how far we've come,
and how we can do better,
What America Means to Me.

I'm nervous even though Mr. Hernandez
has been telling us,
Just have fun,
think of it as a practice run
for regionals next week.

I wait for them to call my name.
I'm outside,
next to the open field behind the MP room.

I wait with the weeds and the wildflowers,
and it's not so clear what is a weed

and what is a flower
in this untamed meadow.

I see the mountain in the near distance.
And underneath the overwhelming sky,
I see a canopy of blue
the same color as the distant sea.

The blue of memory,
the words,
Live a big life.
Dream big dreams.

And the promise,
I will.

Afterword

Land of Broken Promises is a fictional story based on my life. Even though some of the details are made up, so many things are true: my mother did go away to work at a family friend's store (not just for one summer but two), my parents did buy a blue Buick, and between 1981 and 1986, I lived in the United States as an undocumented immigrant.

When President Ronald Reagan signed into law the Immigration Reform and Control Act of 1986, he granted an estimated 2.7 million people the ability to apply for temporary legal status. My family was granted amnesty, and in 1996, I became a United States citizen.

Acknowledgments

It takes a village to publish a book and I'm so grateful for those in my village.

Thanks Jenn Laughran, amazing agent extraordinaire. Thank you to the increasingly brilliant Alexandra Cooper. Thanks Kathy Lam, for the gorgeous book design. Thank you, Julia Kuo, for the absolutely stunning cover art.

Thanks to Allison Weintraub and the entire team at HarperCollins: Rye White, Valerie Shea, Kimberly Craskey, Josh Weiss, Erin Fitzsimmons, David Curtis, and Rosemary Brosnan.

To my readers, those who checked out my book from the library, or bought a copy, or left a nice-ish review or told others about my book, thank you!

Thank you, Debby Lin, Rong Xia and Jack Sung for your legal expertise in immigration law.

Thank you to my friends and family who have always been so quick to offer a word of encouragement. Thanks for all the posts and retweets and for coming to my book launch parties.

Thank you, Linda, for your help and support. This is your story too.

Thank you to my kids for being proud of me. I'm proud of you, too.

Thank you to my husband, my number one fan, my biggest supporter (in more ways than one), and the second greatest love of my life (so far).

Thank you, Mom and Dad, for all the ways you've loved me my whole life.

And to the girl with dove's eyes, thank you for being there.